P9-CEN-775

SATO
THE RABBIT

YUKI AINOYA

TRANSLATED FROM JAPANESE
BY MICHAEL BLASKOWSKY

Enchanted Lion Books
NEW YORK

One day, Haneru Sato became a rabbit.

He's been a rabbit ever since.

He likes stars, the ocean, and tasty treats. He likes lots of other things, too.

What is Sato doing today? What is he going to do tomorrow? 🐰

A TINY POND

Sato the Rabbit is watering plants
in the garden with a very long hose.
Where is the water coming from?

Go around the house …

...and walk into the forest behind it.

Haneru Sato
#2 Forest Way

Continue on through the woods …

… and into the meadow. Beyond the meadow,
there is a small pond …

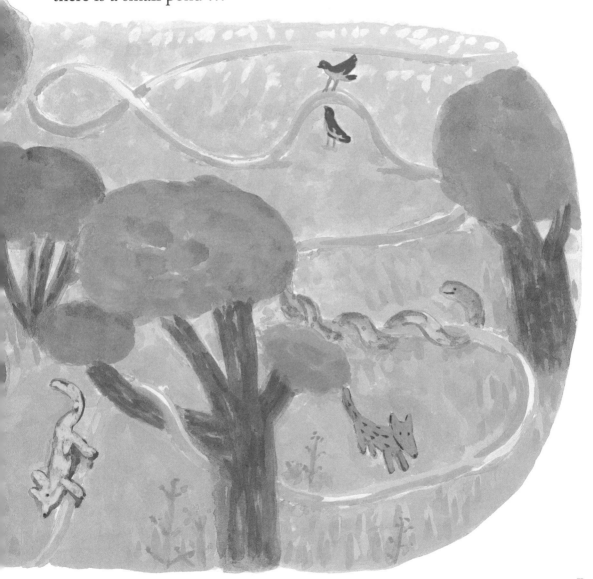

... that is blowing water into the hose as hard as it can.

On the other side of the woods, water shoots up into the sky and forms a tiny rainbow.

It's a sign from Sato that he's finished watering.

The pond goes back to being its tiny, peaceful self.

11

A SEA OF GRASS

On a bright and windy day, Sato the Rabbit washes a lot of laundry.

In a wide open field, he hangs it up piece by piece.

Whoosh! The wind whips through the laundry and the tall green grass.

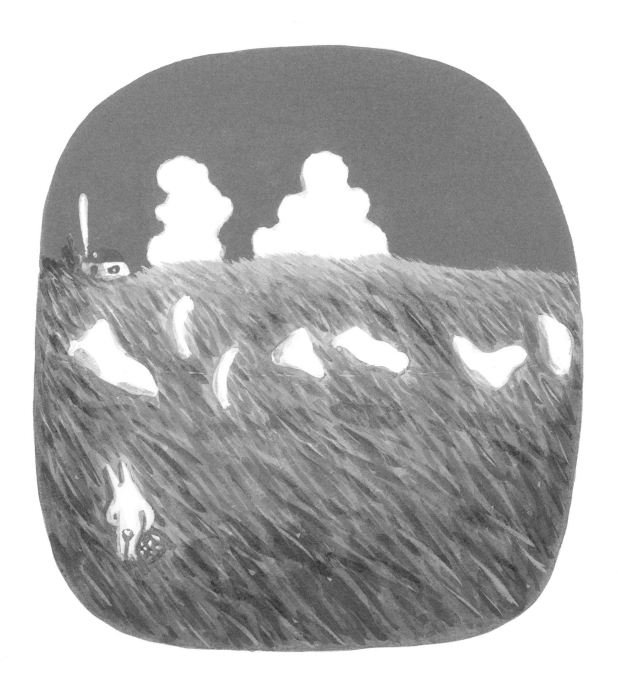

15

17

A perfect gust of wind arrives.
Sato becomes a ship and sets sail
through rippling waves of grass
that carry him far and wide.

A NIGHT OF STARS

On a moonless night, Sato
travels to an observatory
on the peak of a mountain.

He waits in the observatory for a meteor shower.

The meteor shower arrives.

He collects star after star in the dome of the observatory.

Thanks to Sato's stars, it's very bright, even on a moonless night. 🐰

WATERMELON

Sato the Rabbit
is cutting a watermelon.

He places one half on a shelf, then takes his first bite.

The sweet, refreshing taste of watermelon fills his mouth.

It spreads from his mouth
throughout his entire body.

Sato opens his eyes
to take another bite …

… and is standing on a gigantic, floating watermelon.

There's nothing better than
eating watermelon on the sea.

He eats some more
after going for a swim.

As the sun sets, the watermelon is almost gone.

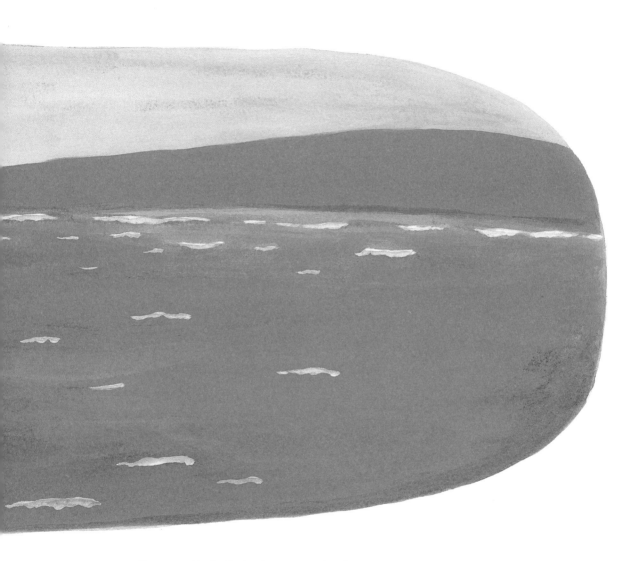

Sato will definitely come back tomorrow
with the other half of the watermelon boat. ♡

A WINDOW TO THE SKY

The rain stops while Sato the Rabbit is out on an evening stroll.

There are a lot of puddles.
Every puddle reflects the clear, vibrant sky.

Sato finds an especially
luminous puddle …

... and tries opening it.

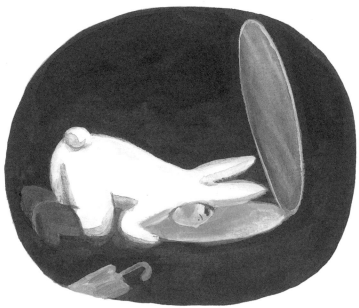

Now Sato waits for another rainy day to find the next window to the sky. 🐰

WALNUTS

Sato the Rabbit
loves walnuts.
He opens the shell
with a *crack* ...

… and finds a tasty nut.

Sometimes the walnuts have especially wonderful things inside.

Crack! He opens the next walnut slowly, so as not to damage the shell.

This walnut has shelves of delicious bread on one side,
and fragrant hot coffee on the other.

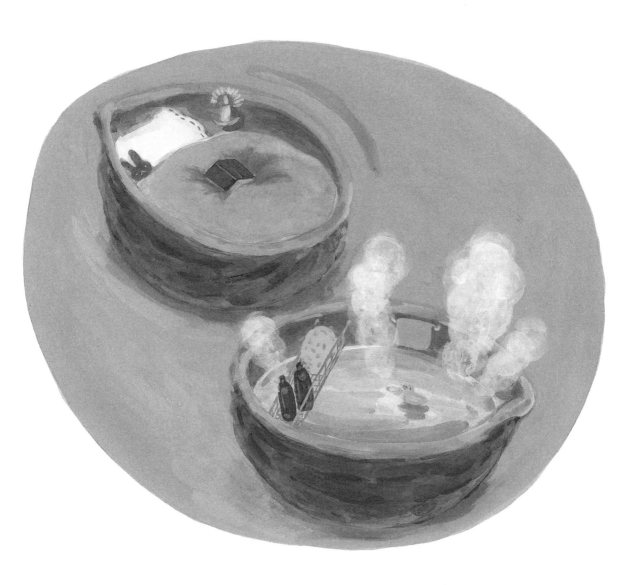

There's a warm bath and a comfy bed in another.

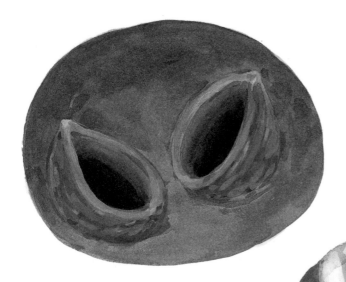

The insides of one walnut
are as dark as a cave.

So he covers his eyes
like this.

It's pitch black at first,
but after a little while …

… it becomes a sky filled with stars.

FOREST ICE

One cold winter morning,
Sato sets out into the forest.

There, he collects ice
from small hollows in
the forest floor where
water trickles through.

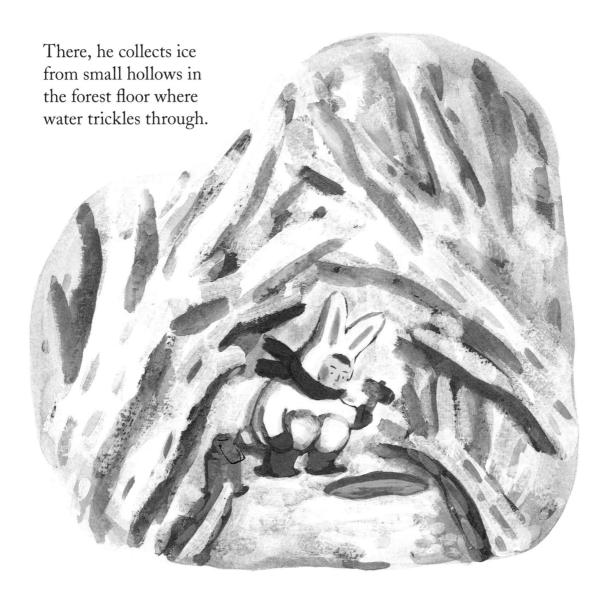

The ice in the forest comes in many colors.

This is because it is made from water containing all the events of spring, summer, and fall.

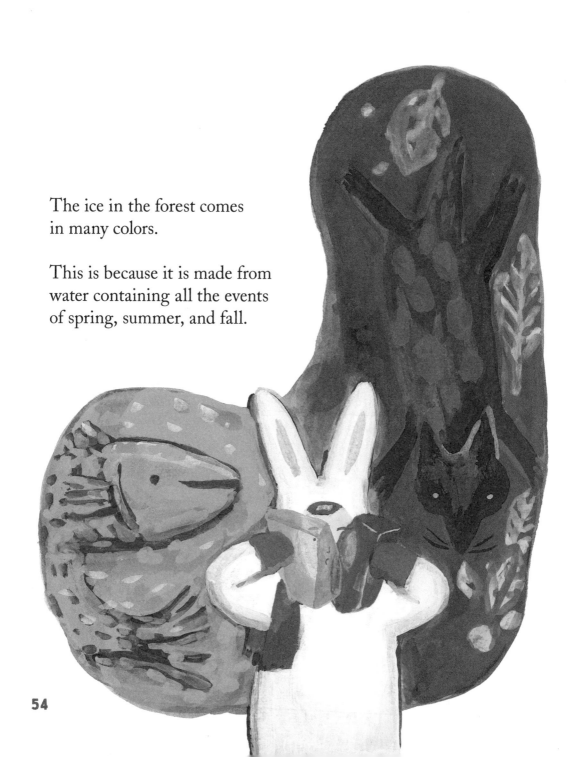

Returning home, Sato drinks a glass of cold tea made with blue ice.

Sorrow is frozen into this ice, giving it a sad flavor.

He melts some orange ice and
a happy aura fills the room.

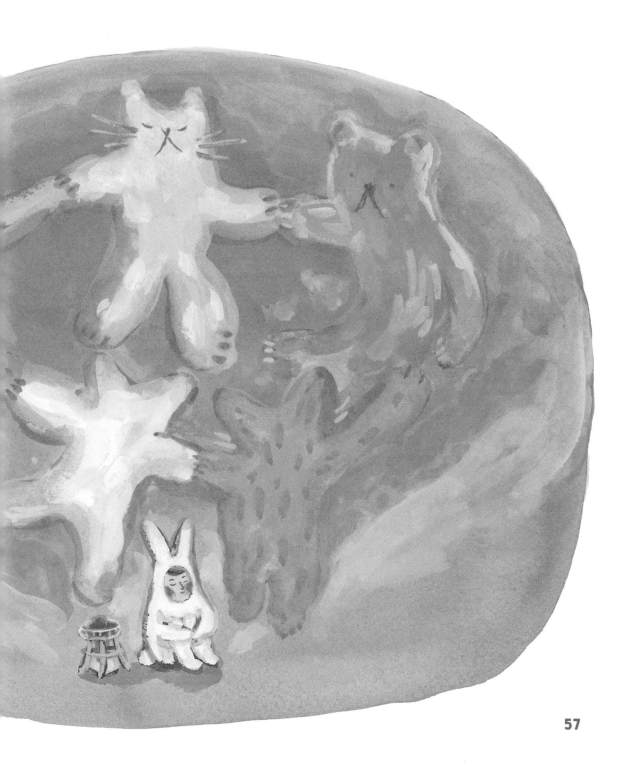

But what Sato likes best of all is floating a little ice of each color in milk and drinking it.

As each piece of ice slowly melts, Sato enjoys sipping stories late into the night. 🐰

www.enchantedlion.com

First English-language edition published in 2021 by Enchanted Lion Books,
248 Creamer Street, Studio 4, Brooklyn, NY 11231
Copyright © 2021 by Enchanted Lion Books for the English-language translation
Editors for the English-language edition: Shizuka Blaskowsky and Claudia Zoe Bedrick
All rights reserved under International and Pan-American Copyright Conventions

USAGI NO SATO-KUN by Yuki AINOYA
Copyright © 2006 Yuki AINOYA
All rights reserved.
Original Japanese edition published by SHOGAKUKAN.
English translation rights arranged with SHOGAKUKAN
through Japan Uni Agency, Inc.

Library of Congress Cataloging Number 2020008527
ISBN 978-1-59270-318-0

Printed in Italy by Società Editoriale Grafiche AZ

First Edition